REBECCA LISLE
Planimal Magic

Joe is staying with his cousins in the
country where his uncle runs a scientific
research institute. Late at night there's a
terrible, heart-stopping wail coming from
outside. Who – or what – is making it?

When Joe, his psychic dog, Bingo,
and cousin, Molly, embark on a search,
they make a magical, mysterious
discovery which some people will do
anything to keep secret ...

First published 2003 by
A & C Black Publishers Ltd
37 Soho Square, London, W1D 3QZ

www.acblack.com

Copyright © 2003 Rebecca Lisle

ISBN 0-7136-6656-0

A CIP catalogue for this book is available from the British Library.

Printed and bound in Spain by G. Z. Printek, Bilbao.

REBECCA LISLE

Planimal Magic

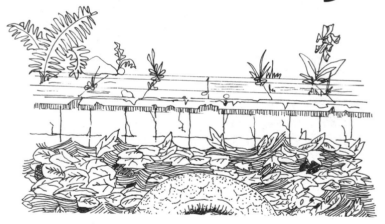

with illustrations by the author

A & C Black • London

For Tommy and Maxi Brigden

Chapter One
Night Noises

Joe woke suddenly.

What had he heard?

The weird sound had gone, but something of it still lingered in his head like a shadow.

Joe lay very still, listening, arms straight at his sides. That reminded him of his mother. Then he remembered he wasn't at home, and opened his eyes.

The noise again! Something in the garden. A terrible cry: a heart-stopping, nerve-tingling wail. Animal, but what animal made a noise like that?

'Bingo?'

Bingo's snoring stopped abruptly, there was a pause, then he scrambled on to the bed beside Joe.

'Good boy,' whispered Joe, wrapping his arm

around him. 'That's better.'

Sliding his other hand under his pillow, Joe closed his fingers around his mum's last present to him. Magic dice.

'Black and white like Bingo and just as lucky!' she'd said.

Mum, Mum … and suddenly Joe was sliding through time, back to his last talk with his dad.

'Mum'll miss you while you're at your cousin's.'

'She won't even notice,' said Joe, gloomily. 'She doesn't care.'

'Joe. Don't say that!'

'If she cared she'd get out of bed. Can't you just *make* Mum get up?'

'How? For God's sake, how?'

Joe's mum had had cancer. She was OK now, only she couldn't quite believe it and the only place she felt safe was in her bed.

'Listen, I'm sorry I shouted,' said his dad. 'You go to Molly's. I'll try and get the place tidied up, maybe even get to work on that garden – so when you come back things'll be better and Mum'll want to get up. OK?'

* * *

Joe sat up in bed. I *must* stop thinking about home, he chided himself. Molly asked me to come. I need to think about her.

Late next morning, he and Bingo made their

way down the wide, panelled stairway to the kitchen.

The kitchen was vast, with a high dusty ceiling. Old biscuit tins were piled haphazardly on top of the cupboards, labelled, 'curtain hooks', 'fuse wire', 'pegs' and such like, but Joe was pretty certain they were empty.

The two enormous windows were covered with glass shelves packed with potted plants. Leaves trailed around the windows and clung to the light fittings.

'There's only porridge or toast,' said Molly, making a funny face. 'You know Dad, he still thinks cornflakes are modern.'

Molly's dad, Dr Robert Martin, was a scientist, who, although forward-thinking in science, was very backward-thinking in other areas.

Joe grinned. 'Doctor's orders, eh?' When Molly didn't return his grin Joe chewed his toast thoughtfully. 'So, what's up, Mol?' he said.

Molly twisted her long straw-coloured hair round and round her fingers.

'Well …' she began.

Joe threw his last crust for Bingo who leapt up and caught it.

'Come on, Mol, before Bingo, the only psychic dog in England, tells me all.'

He waited, noticing that the jam he'd been spreading on his toast had discs of white furry mould on it. Just like home.

'Woof! Woof! Woof!'

Bingo's sudden bark was right by Joe and he jumped up, knocked his coffee over and sent his chair crashing to the floor.

'Oh, Bingo! Now look what I've done!'

Chapter Two
Bingo Blunders

It was just Dr Martin.

'Hi, kids. Everything all right, Joe?' he asked, stepping over the chair.

'Hello. Shush Bingo. It's Uncle Rob.'

Sheepishly, Bingo wagged his tail and slunk over to Molly's dad.

'Herrum, good dog, Bingo,' said Uncle Rob, rubbing his ears. 'Any coffee going? Preferably not that I have to lick off the table,' he added, peering at the brown pool. '*Is* that coffee?' he asked, changing his glasses for another pair.

'Sorry, Uncle Rob.' Joe mopped up the mess.

Dr Martin was in charge of the Centre for Botanical Research, which he ran from their house in Somerset. He was small and bony with a lot of thick grey hair, a long chin and spider-leg fingers. When Uncle Rob had picked Joe up from the station last night he'd hardly spared him a look or a word. He seemed more preoccupied than ever.

'Herrum,' began Dr Martin, squinting through his straggly hair and thick lenses. 'Glad you could keep Molly company. The Research Centre's so busy: our students, Imelda and Bryan, are staying through the holiday. Mrs McBride will be in to cook – if you can call it that – as usual. Now, what else? Did I ask you how your parents are?'

Joe nodded, not wanting to go into it again.

'Herrum, so,' went on Uncle Rob, 'still doing magic?'

Joe smiled. 'Yeah.'

'Good. Herrum, ah, good coffee, Joe ...' He picked up a scientific journal absent-mindedly and flicked through it. 'I seem to remember, some of your tricks actually worked.'

'Oh, thanks, Uncle Rob!'

The back door opened and Bingo burst out barking again. There were shuffles and feet-wiping noises in the lobby, then the kitchen door opened and the two white-coated students came in. Bingo's barking rose to a frenzy.

Joe grabbed his collar. 'For goodness' sake, Bingo!'

The male student pretended to be frightened.

'Aagh! It's going for my jugular!' he cried, staggering and clutching his throat. 'It's after my blood.'

'No, no, he isn't!' Joe assured him.

'Oh, all right, then,' laughed the man. 'Any coffee?'

'Shut *up*, Bingo,' Joe hissed, clamping his hand around Bingo's jaws.

'Maybe he doesn't like the white coats,' Molly suggested.

Dr Martin introduced Joe to the students.

'And I am Imelda,' said the woman, giving Bingo a wide berth. 'Good mornink. Yes?'

Joe blinked. He felt as if someone had just whacked him over the head with a mallet. He stared dumbfounded at Imelda. He'd never seen *anyone* like her before. He'd read about girls being so beautiful they took your breath away, and now – *gasp, gasp* – here it was, happening to *him*.

Imelda was fantastic. Joe stared and stared. Her shining, billowing mass of silvery-gold hair reached almost to her waist. Her face was heart-shaped with a tiny, sharp-tipped nose. Her pale green eyes were fringed with black lashes, the whites as white as icing sugar. Her lips were incredibly full and red and, and—

Joe forced himself to look away – only to find Molly staring fiercely at him.

A blush swept hotly over his face.

Whoops!

Bryan tried to pat Bingo, but the little dog sniffed him, got up and walked away with his nose in the air.

Dr Martin laughed. 'He's sensitive, isn't he, Joe? Is that from helping with all those magic tricks?'

'What sort of magic?' asked Bryan.

'Oh, you know …'

Joe had been tantalised by Imelda's beauty, now he was knocked out by Bryan's ugliness.

Bryan's pale, knobbly face was just like an artichoke and although he couldn't have been very old, his string-coloured hair was sparse and thin. He had red-rimmed eyes, brown teeth and a lop-sided smile that made him look half-witted.

'Bingo is a psychic …' said Joe.

'What? A side-kick?' Bryan laughed.

'No, no, a *psychic*. He can read minds. Innermost thoughts.'

'I would be hopink not *my* thoughts,' said Imelda, darkly.

'Oh, I love your accent,' Joe blurted. 'Where are you from, Imelda?'

'Ah, Joe, I am not foreign. I had an accident, a very bad accident and I am not beink the same since ever. My speech was affected by it … other things too …' she added, her green eyes locking on to his.

Joe blushed. 'Sorry, I …'

'That's all right, Joe,' she smiled.

Bryan interrupted. 'Go on, then, how d'you do your tricks?'

'I am a magician,' Joe said, standing up and flourishing an imaginary cloak, 'and cannot divulge my secrets.'

'Ah, go on,' said Bryan, leaning back in his chair.

'No, really …'

'Please, for me,' said Imelda. 'I am lovink all the magical things.'

'OK,' Joe said. 'Bingo, tricks?'

Immediately alert, the little dog scampered over and sat at his feet.

'Ready, Bingo?'

Bingo sat back on his haunches, front paws off the ground.

'OK. Bingo, *counting*! How many people can you see?'

Bingo looked round the kitchen. 'Bark. Bark. Bark. Bark.' Four barks.

Then Bingo sat down again.

'*Bingo*,' Joe hissed, frantically giving him the signal to bark. 'Bingo, Bingo …' But Bingo slipped under the table and licked his tummy.

Bryan spluttered into his coffee. 'Brilliant, Mr Magician! Fantastic! Only there are *five* of us in the room. Can't he count more than four?'

'He usually gets it right,' Joe muttered.

'He does, honestly,' agreed Molly. Her eyes were glistening. 'Bingo's really clever.'

'It is only an animal,' Imelda said in a strange, fierce, quiet voice. 'But … I have never been able to understand what people is findink so interestink in animals.' She smiled brilliantly at Joe. 'They are smellink and lickink with their tongues and are so dirty. I am not happy in particular to have this animal in the kitchen where we have food.'

Steel fingers wrapped around Joe's heart and squeezed. She didn't like his dear Bingo!

'But …' Joe looked from Molly to Uncle Rob for help.

'Imelda's right,' said Bryan, rubbing his knobbly chin. 'Full of germs, dogs are.'

'Herrum, er, perhaps not in the kitchen, then,' said Dr Martin, getting up and ignoring the pleading look Molly threw him. He took out a pair of glasses and swapped them with the pair on his nose, as if able to think better that way. 'We must consider Imelda's feelings.'

As Joe and Molly took Bingo out, Molly whispered angrily, 'Feelings? Imelda hasn't got any feelings.'

Chapter Three
Fertiliser

'You big nit!' hissed Molly, when they were alone in the garden. 'How *could* you, Joe?'

'What?'

'You know! Fall for her! For her silly voice and glittery eyes. Especially when she was so horrid about Bingo.'

'Oh, well,' said Joe, shrugging. 'Bingo won't mind.'

'*I* mind! She can't make rules here!'

'No, I know ... Odd Bingo got his trick wrong,' mused Joe. 'He never has before ...'

'Maybe he fell for her charms, too? You should look at her more closely next time, Joe. She's not what she seems. I think she's had a facelift.'

'Really? Where was her face before? Round

her ankles?'

Molly couldn't suppress a giggle. 'Silly! Have a close look next time. I'm sure there's a sort of tuck by her ears. And her skin looks so tight.'

'Perhaps it was that terrible accident she told us about, her face was all messed up, and she needed plastic surgery. Maybe,' went on Joe, warming to the idea, 'a dog caused the accident and so she's hated dogs ever since.'

'Brilliant!' laughed Molly.

They sat down on a bench. Joe watched Bingo snuffling about in the flowerbeds. His garden at home was nothing compared to this. The lawns were not even green.

Joe was about to say something about the garden when he saw Molly surreptitiously mopping at her eyes with the ends of her hair.

'Now, Mol, come on,' said Joe, gently, 'tell me what's up. Don't cry.' He pulled Molly's letter out of his pocket, uncreased it, and read …

> Please, please come, Joe, I can't bear it a moment longer and I'm worried something horrible is going on.

'So what is it?'

'It's everything,' Molly explained. 'Honestly, I'm like a stranger in my own home these days. I'm not allowed in the lab. Mustn't answer the phone. Mustn't ask any questions. Mustn't open closed doors. Don't touch this, don't touch that! Even the pool's out of bounds.'

'Bad,' Joe made a face. 'I'm sorry.' He had a sudden idea to try and cheer her up. 'Look,' he said, digging into his pocket. 'Mum got these for me. It was, like, the last time she was interested in my tricks, so they're extra special. Magic dice. Go on, have a go.'

Molly rolled the dice across the bench and got two sixes. She did it again: two sixes.

'Clever.' She smiled weakly.

'Yeah, specially when I do this.' Joe took the dice, blew on them and handed them back to her.

Molly shook the dice and threw. Two ones.

'Oh!' she cried. 'How d'you do that?'

'Magic,' said Joe, grinning slyly. 'They're my favourite because they *always* work ... Now, for my next trick ...' he said handing her a small velvet bag. 'An empty bag.'

'Yes, empty,' agreed Molly, giving it back.

'But when I say the magic words, *Spink spank, skiddle skaddle, up the Khyber without a paddle,* a mouse will appear!'

Joe twirled the bag and spun it into Molly's hands. She peeped inside.

'Empty,' she said, tipping it upside down.

Joe grabbed the bag. 'It can't be! *It is!* That's the second mouse I've lost this week! When you think of all the magicians' mice that must be disappearing every day … hundreds … thousands. Where are they?'

He looked so forlorn, Molly couldn't help smiling. 'They'll turn up one day, when you least expect it.'

'Maybe.'

They sat in silence for a whole minute. Then Molly said, 'I'm truly worried.'

'I can see,' said Joe.

'But I didn't tell you the worst. You know I said they've locked the pool? Well, they're *doing* something in there,' she whispered. 'I heard something …'

'What?'

'Splashing.'

'Imelda having a swim?'

It was a joke. Joe knew the stagnant pool was full of leaves and the water was freezing cold. Nobody had swum in it for years.

'Seriously, I think it was an animal,' said Molly. 'But Joe, they're *botanists*, they shouldn't have an animal in there.'

Immediately, Joe recalled the strange, haunting noise he'd heard in the night. He shivered, not wanting to remember that sad sound.

'Joe, the World's Jolliest Magician, will help you!' he said cheerfully. 'We'll investigate. We'll assert ourselves, you know, make a stand or something … Don't worry. Now, where's that bad dog of mine?'

* * *

The Centre for Botanical Research consisted of a big Victorian house, three old greenhouses and two long barns which had been converted into a laboratory, all set in a large rambling overgrown garden.

'I bet Bingo's there,' said Molly, pointing at the greenhouses. 'Voles and field mice sneak inside 'cos it's so warm.'

'Maybe my mice are in there,' said Joe, eagerly.

As they got close to the long greenhouses they saw notices had been pinned to the doors …

EXPERIMENT IN PROGRESS:
NO ADMITTANCE

'See! Just look at that!' said Molly, angrily. She chewed on her hair. 'More experiments! But I wouldn't touch anything – why would I? Everyone's got so uptight here.'

'They can't mind if we just nip in for a mo …' whispered Joe, slipping inside. 'Bingo! Here, boy!'

Walking into the greenhouse was like walking into a jungle. Two long wooden shelves ran the length of the building and they were packed with potted plants whose leaves and stems intertwined across the high glass ceiling. The air was warm and moist.

Molly breathed deeply. 'I love it.'

'Smells so green,' agreed Joe, sniffing. 'And here's Bingo.' He slipped the dog on to the lead.

'Look!' hissed Molly, suddenly grabbing Joe's arm. 'It's Bryan in the next greenhouse. Hide!'

They crouched below the shelf and peered through the greenery.

'He's drinking fertiliser!' hissed Joe. 'Mum uses that stuff in the garden.'

'Wouldn't fertiliser be poisonous? It must be something else … D'you think he's got brandy in there? Or gin?'

'Or vodka,' said Joe. 'My mate Pete's dad's an alcoholic and he drinks vodka. He says it looks like water and hasn't got much smell. D'you reckon Bryan's an alcoholic?'

'Don't know. But he is sick sometimes …'

'Your Dad might fire him if he was an alcoholic.'

'Brilliant idea! He might!'

'We'd better make sure that's what he *is* doing,' said Joe, reasonably. 'It may be water.'

They waited for Bryan to go, then sneaked into the adjacent greenhouse.

'Look, here's the bottle.' Molly reached in amongst the plants. 'It smells disgusting,' she groaned, sniffing it. 'You try.'

'Urgh! Dead things. Old drains,' said Joe, reeling and clutching at his throat. 'No one could drink that.'

'No wonder he's been ill. Pour a bit out.'

Joe was just tipping out the last few drops of thick vibrant yellow liquid, when they heard a noise and spun round guiltily.

'*Hey!* What d'you think you're doing!'

Bryan blocked the doorway.

'Nothing!' Joe put the bottle down sharply.

'Get out of here!' Bryan roared, striding towards them, his white coat flapping like wings. 'You're not allowed. We've *told* you.'

Molly had gone as pale as a sheet of paper and looked like she would fold up and fall down there and then. Joe gulped and grinned and waved his arms around.

'A bird was trapped,' he lied quickly. 'We were just shooing it out. Shoo! Shoo!' he added, waving his arms again.

'A bird?'

'A robin,' grinned Joe.

'Where?' Bryan turned to see the imaginary bird.

'There! Oh, it's gone! You missed it.'

By the time Bryan looked back, Joe and Molly were pushing past him and half-way out of the greenhouse.

'And don't come back!' yelled Bryan, as they scampered off down the path.

Chapter Four
Photosynthesis

In the middle of Tuesday night, Joe woke suddenly. It was the same terrible, heartbreaking wail he'd heard the night before. He sat up, clutching his pillow.

'What is it?'

The sound still echoed round his head as he pulled the duvet off the bed, wrapped it around his shoulders and crept along the corridor to Molly's room.

'Mol?'

Molly was kneeling on her bed, looking out of the window. Bingo jumped up beside her.

'Did you hear it?' she asked, turning her pale and worried face to him. She was trembling. 'Wasn't it awful? Almost like a sort of sad song.'

'Yeah,' said Joe, 'but animals don't sing, well birds do, I suppose.'

'It wasn't a bird ...'

'No. Rabbits scream. Have you ever heard one stuck in a trap? Horrible. It wasn't a rabbit.'

'What's out there, d'you think?'

'I don't know.'

'The students are hurting it,' she gulped.

She couldn't help the pictures in her mind, things she'd seen on anti-vivisection posters: cats, with their heads cut open, brain exposed; horrible things.

'That thing needs help, Joe, it does.'

'And we'll help it, Mol. We've got to get into that pool first. Therein lies the root of this enigma,' he said mysteriously. 'That's from one of my magic books.'

'Your magic books don't know the place is locked up,' said Molly.

'Then let's sneak into the lab.'

'They lock that up, too.'

'What about your dad's office? His office in the house?'

'Locked.'

Joe made a face. 'Hey, this is beginning to sound serious, but we'll do it. I promise we will.'

Back in his bed, Joe let Bingo tuck his nose up close, despite his bad breath. How could anyone hurt an animal? Joe wondered, stroking Bingo's silky head. How *could* they?

* * *

In the kitchen next morning, Mrs McBride was panicking.

'Six!' she cried, twisting her hands round and round in her apron. 'First lunch for five and now lunch for six and Professor Leef is a big man ... I'll have to get more carrots, now,' she said, going out.

'Who's Professor Leef?' asked Joe.

'Dad's new boss,' said Molly. 'He's in charge of funding the Research Centre so we have to be nice to him. But *he* gave us Imelda. He's to blame for overworking Dad. The big bully. Big smooth, soft, pink milkshake of a bully!'

Joe hooted with laughter and was just imitating what he thought a human milkshake might look like, when Uncle Rob and the students came in.

'Whoops ...' Joe swiftly picked up a potted plant and sniffed its flowers.

'What are you doing, Joe?'

'Just admiring your flowers, Uncle Rob.'

'Odd boy,' muttered Bryan.

'Tell me, Uncle Rob,' said Joe, glaring at Bryan, 'what is it that's so great about plants?'

'They're food for insects,' snapped Bryan, picking a caterpillar off his sleeve. 'All these plants: I'm crawling with caterpillars. And green fly!'

Imelda laid a hand comfortingly on his shoulder. 'There, there,' she said. 'You are being so attractive to them, like the ways what you are to me.'

'I mean,' went on Joe, 'how are they important?'

Dr Martin shot into the air as though he'd sat on a pin. 'Joe, Joe! What do they teach you in school these days?'

Joe grinned. 'Not a lot.'

'So it seems. What did we have for lunch yesterday?'

'Pizza,' said Joe, still grinning. That was easy, he thought.

'And what was the pizza made of?'

'Cheese and tomato and stuff.'

'OK. The "stuff" is dough. What's dough made from?'

'Flour?' Joe suggested.

'And what's flour made from?'

'Er, wheat?' Joe said.

'Yes,' said Dr Martin nodding his head. 'And Joe, what is wheat?'

'It's just wheat,' said Joe. 'I mean, you know, it's a plant ...'

'Exactly. Wheat is a green plant. I know it's yellow when you see it, but it starts life green.

There were tomatoes on the pizza, too. They grow on a *green* plant.'

'So? I mean, yeah, well …'

'I'm trying to tell you that plants are important. You depend on plants for your food, Joe. All of it.'

'Well …' Joe heard Bryan sniggering and glared fiercely at him.

'And your feet, Joe, what's on your feet?' said Uncle Rob.

'They were trainers once,' Joe said, 'honest. But they were never plants.'

'But they *are* leather, Joe, and leather comes from?'

'Cows,' said Joe and Molly together.

'And cows eat grass. Grass is green, a green plant. Everything comes from plants, depends on plants in one way or another: it's called a food chain.'

Joe made a face. *Everything?* It didn't seem possible. He looked round the room: the table was made of wood and wood came from trees, they were plants. Apples on the table: plants. But the kettle? – that had never had any organic connections.

'What about steel and plastic and stuff? Glass? Polystyrene tiles? Fibreglass?' cried Joe.

'Yes,' said Dr Martin, 'not plants, but made by people, and people have to eat to work and as

I've just explained, all food originally comes from green plants.'

'And there's oxygen,' said Molly.

'I thought you were on my side,' said Joe, miserably.

'I am,' she laughed. 'We need oxygen to breathe.'

'I do know that,' Joe said. 'What d'you think I am? Dumb or something?'

'The idea never crossed my mind,' said Bryan coldly.

Joe didn't like the way he said that.

'I remember,' he said, racking his brain. 'Plants use up the carbon dioxide when they do that photosynthesis thing, and produce oxygen. We need them for that.'

Dr Martin laughed. 'That's right. We get chemicals from plants too. So you see, plants are important. Without them we just couldn't exist.'

'And they're beautiful,' said Molly. 'And some smell nice.'

'OK,' Joe agreed. 'But,' he whispered to Molly, 'they're still dull.'

'We'll make a scientist of you yet,' said Dr Martin, retreating to his office.

Imelda made some tea and a few minutes later, she and Bryan went out. As they went over to the lab, Bryan called, 'Here, Bingo!' and threw something.

The little dog leapt in the air, caught it, then immediately spat it out with a dreadful howl. Bryan watched him coldly.

'What is it?' Joe was beside him in seconds.

Bingo was shaking his head from side to side, yelping and pawing at his mouth.

'What?'

Then he saw. Bryan had tossed him his boiling hot tea bag. It lay steaming on the ground beside them.

'You rat!' cried Joe.

'Oh, dear, oh dear,' said Bryan in mock sympathy. 'Was it a bit hot? Did his psychic powers abandon him?'

Smirking, he followed Imelda into the lab.

'I'm going to tell Dad,' said Molly. 'They can't do that.'

Joe's eyes were smarting with tears. 'Poor, poor, Bingo,' he said, hugging him. 'It's OK, boy.'

When Molly came out of the house again, she looked shocked. She walked unsteadily over to Joe.

'I can't believe it,' she said in a choked voice. 'Dad said it was high spirits. Just their idea of fun.'

'He ...? Oh, never mind. Don't worry. Nothing too serious.'

Molly didn't need anything more to worry about.

'I hope you noticed how Imelda didn't come rushing to Bingo's aid?' Molly asked.

'Yes,' agreed Joe, thoughtfully, 'I did. And if they could do that to Bingo, they could do something so much worse to an animal behind locked doors, couldn't they?'

Chapter Five
Not a Fish

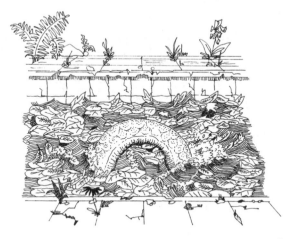

That afternoon, when Professor Leef, the students and Uncle Rob were all busy in the laboratory, Molly and Joe set off for the swimming pool. They planned to climb over the wall at the point furthest from the house.

They made their way through the tangle of trees and bushes and falling-down sheds housing ancient machinery, to the most distant part of the garden. Molly hardly spoke.

Joe guessed Molly felt Uncle Rob had let her down. Same as Mum and Dad have let me down, thought Joe. Dad should make Mum get up and *make* her positive again – now she's on the mend and everything. Parents shouldn't be allowed just to give in if they want their kids to respect them! When I'm a dad I won't let my kids down.

'Just past the old garage,' said Molly, 'where that stone shed is against the pool wall. We can go over there.'

Joe turned over a wheelbarrow to climb on. 'It'll be easy,' he said, pulling himself on to the roof.

Abruptly, Bingo started barking.

'Maybe he's sensing danger. I mean, he is psychic, isn't he, Joe?' said Molly, trying to be cheerful.

'Huh, he hasn't shown much sign of it recently,' said Joe. 'Hush boy. Sit!'

Quickly, Molly followed Joe and soon they both lay across the wet, mossy roof slates.

'What am I so scared of?' whispered Molly.

'Don't know, but I'm scared of it too,' said Joe.

They pushed through the branches of a pear tree.

'Can you see anything?' hissed Molly. 'These twigs are trying to poke me in the eye.'

'No, they're not,' Joe grinned. 'They're shielding us. Plants are important. They hide us from our enemies and give us oxygen. Plants are our friends.'

'Don't make me giggle! I'll fall!'

A fine rain began as they inched their way to the top of the sloping roof and peered down at the water below.

There was something about the pool that gave it a prehistoric feel, as if nothing had disturbed it for years and years, thought Joe. Perhaps it was because the paved area around the water was overgrown with giant weeds, bracken and moss. Or maybe it was that the air trapped within the four walls was so totally still.

The only sounds were the dull lapping noise of the water and the patter of the drizzle falling on the carpet of grey blossom which covered the water's surface.

'Spooky,' breathed Joe.

'Yeah, spooky and weird,' whispered Molly.

The rain began to fall harder, dripping from the branches and splashing on the roof. Below them, Bingo started a low rumbling growl and barked softly, warningly, but Joe hardly heard him; he was scanning the water's surface for any movement. It was perfectly still. Nothing was stirring. No sound except the rain.

'Look!' cried Molly, grabbing at Joe so suddenly that the shock set his heart thumping crazily.

'Where? What?'

'Something's under the leaves. See?'

Joe felt his senses sharpen and intensify, as if a gear had shifted inside his head: the cold rain seeping down his neck; the hard edge of the wall pressing into his knee; a tiny bit of rough concrete under his left hand and a creeping sensation which rippled over his scalp. Fear. Panic. His stomach seemed to push up into his throat so he could hardly speak.

'There's something there! Quite big ...' he gasped.

'Fish?' Molly's voice cracked.

'No, not a fish.'

'No, not a fish,' Molly repeated.

'What, then? I never thought there'd *be* something, not really.'

The leaves shifted, sliding over one another, showing the murky black water below.

Joe blinked the rain from his eyes. 'There! Did you see that?' He scrambled upright, floundering on the wet tiles. 'Mol! Look at that! It's ... Oh! Ouch!'

His left foot slipped and he fell with a crash against the tiles. He grabbed for a handhold, missed and shot backwards, sliding fast into the tree.

Below them, Bingo barked and barked.

Everything was happening too quickly. Just as Joe saw the thing in the pool and lost his footing, he registered Bingo's bark.

'Someone's coming! Get down, quick!'

They slipped the rest of the way and dropped down on to the ground.

'Good dog! Come boy, come!'

'To the garage,' gasped Molly, dodging through the trees.

They slid quickly in through the gap in the sagging wooden doors and immediately fell still and silent.

The *thump thump* of their hearts rang in their ears. Joe held Bingo in his arms, whispering soothing words in his ear as he watched.

It was Imelda. She stopped by the upturned wheelbarrow, stared at the flattened grass, the shoe marks on the side of the shed.

Joe and Molly held their breath, willing her not to look towards the garage and somehow she didn't. She spun on her heel and went swiftly back the way she'd come.

They were safe. For now.

Chapter Six

Juggling Joe's Magic Show

'So what did you see?' asked Molly.

'What did *you* see?' asked Joe, avoiding her eyes.

They'd gone back to the house and taken refuge in the old music room where an ancient grand piano and harp gathered dust. There were three big windows draped with thick velvet curtains and deep cushions on the seats. Nobody ever went in there except them.

Molly sank further into the corner of the window seat and wrapped the bottom of the thick curtain round her still damp legs. She gathered Bingo on to her knee and stroked his ears.

'I only got a glimpse ...'

Their eyes met over the edge of the curtain.

'Was it sort of greenish?'

'Yes.'

'With a long neck?'

'Yes.'

'Like a … it's stupid, but like a *dinosaur*.'

'Heck,' said Joe. He took out his dice and tossed them thoughtfully.

'Just what I was thinking,' said Molly. 'And somewhere,' said Molly, unwinding the curtain, 'I've got a picture.'

She soon returned, bringing a large picture book of dinosaurs.

'There!' she said, pointing to a drawing of a large aquatic creature. 'Was it like that? That's a plesiosaur.'

'I dunno, I hardly saw it,' said Joe. 'I was falling down the roof, but yes – only green.'

'This one's brown but then the people who wrote the book have never seen a real one – not like us,' said Molly, suddenly grinning. 'They're only guessing about the colour, aren't they?'

Joe breathed out loudly. He rolled his dice: two sixes.

'Phew,' he said.

Molly nodded. 'Dad *can't* know. He'd never let them hurt an animal, would he?'

'No, well, no,' Joe faltered. 'I'm sure he wouldn't. We should tell him.'

'It's just …' she said, awkwardly, chewing on

her thumb. 'If he *does* know ... Oh! Hello, Imelda!'

'*Imelda!*' Joe shot off the seat.

'There you are,' Imelda said, gliding smoothly towards Joe. 'I am wantink to ask you Joe ...' She leant so close her white-blonde hair swished against his cheek, '... to be doing somethink magic for us tonight? You understand what I'm meanink? To show Professor Leef? He is likink magic very much, I know.'

'Er ...'

'You are such a clever boy,' she added. 'Your magic will be workink tonight, I am assured of it.'

Joe couldn't speak. Had she heard them? Was this all an elaborate plan to make them think she hadn't? If she'd so much as heard the word 'dinosaur', they were finished.

He met her eyes: it was like looking at polished glass, no life or warmth at all. Molly was right. The woman was crazy – and mean.

'Of course,' he said brightly. 'I'd love to. That would be fine. Yes.'

'Excellentific!' she said, patting his shoulder. 'See you later.'

Joe and Molly broke into hysterical giggles. They stuffed their hands into their mouths and muffled their heads with the velvet curtains.

'*Excellentific!*' Joe mimicked.

'Awful!'

'Gross!'

'She's sad!'

'Yeah, and she's scary,' said Joe, his giggles drying up suddenly. 'You were right. I don't like her one little bit.'

'But you still think she's pretty?'

Joe grinned, wryly. 'To tell you the truth, I don't. Her skin's too tight. Her teeth are too perfect. And that tiny nose? It's too sharp, like one of those old-fashioned tin openers.'

Molly giggled. 'But you'll still do magic for her?'

'Yeah. Got to. We've got to act like we don't suspect them ... and hope Bingo doesn't play up again.'

* * *

Joe was anxious about his performance, but not reluctant; he loved doing magic shows, loved showing off.

Joe collected his cloak and things from his room. As he raced downstairs, he bumped into Bryan, drinking from the little, brown bottle again.

'What?' Bryan snapped nastily as he slipped the bottle into his pocket. 'What's your problem?'

Joe's brain whirred. It was the same yellow stuff Bryan had been drinking in the greenhouse. What *was* in the bottle? Bryan looked ill; his skin sweaty and yellow like cheese rind.

'No problem,' Joe stammered, hurrying on.

Joe burst into the dining room, flourishing his cloak. Everyone clapped except the Professor who was busy lighting up a cigar.

Rolling leaves up and burning them is hardly kind to plants, Joe thought, darkly, watching the cigar smoke. And it's not kind to us, either.

'Good evening, ladies and gentlemen!' cried Joe, sending three bananas whirling in the air. 'Welcome to Juggling Joe's Magic Show!' The audience clapped. 'For my first trick, my assistant, Bingo, the one and only psychic dog, will read my mind.'

Some of the audience clapped.

Joe was blindfolded while Molly held a pack of cards out to Bingo and Bingo took one with his teeth and showed the audience.

'Bingo is telepathically transferring the picture of the card to me,' Joe explained.

After a few seconds, Bingo began to bark and rumble quietly, as if he was talking.

'The six of clubs!' cried Joe.

Professor Leef clapped. 'Well done!'

Everything went well until his last trick.

'Now, if you would check this velvet bag,' said Joe, offering it to Professor Leef, 'you will find it is entirely empty.'

But for once the bag wasn't empty.

As Professor Leef turned it upside down, a

mouse fell out.

A *green* mouse.

'Ah! I am hatink mouses!' squeaked Imelda.

Bryan yelped.

'Good God!' Dr Martin stood up, knocking over his chair.

'It's green!' said Molly. *'Green?'*

'Catch it!' roared Professor Leef.

But the mouse had already squeezed under the door and disappeared.

'Where did it come from?' said Dr Martin.

Joe looked startled. That was what *he* wanted to know.

'I am hatink mouses,' said Imelda, unwrapping the professor's arms from around her legs and climbing down from the chair where she'd taken refuge. 'I am loathink these creatures more than any other furry bodies. It is my up-brimmink.'

'Upbringing,' Professor Leef corrected her with a chuckle. 'Silly.'

Imelda flashed him a bright smile. 'Upbrinkink,' she repeated. 'Thank you, Professor, how could I make such a mistook? Oh, Bryan,' she added. 'You're as white as a sheep.'

'Sheet,' said Professor Leef. His soft face wobbled with laughter.

'Don't you like mice, either?' Joe asked Bryan. Or was it seeing the Professor with his arms

42

locked round his girlfriend's legs, he wondered.

'Sheet. I am meanink sheet, of course,' said Imelda. 'Bryan, I think you should take more of your vitamins. Come with me. Come, Bryan.' She led him out.

'Well, well,' said Professor Leef, examining the end of his cigar thoughtfully. 'Where did that mouse come from, eh? Robert?'

'I'm in the dark,' Dr Martin said softly, polishing his glasses.

Professor Leef glanced at the two children and nodded to the door. 'Your office?'

'Certainly,' Dr Martin said gruffly, and they went out.

'Ugh! Smoke!' Molly waved her hand through the cigar smoke. 'What was all *that* about? Hey, that green mouse was some trick, Joe!'

'Not *mine*!' said Joe, alarmed. 'I don't know where it came from. I've never seen a green mouse before, ever!'

'Really? That's so weird,' said Molly, stacking the dinner plates on to the trolley. She gazed intently at Joe. 'Because *they* weren't fazed by it, were they? The mouse was green: fur, legs everything, amazing! But did anyone seem surprised? No!'

'So?'

'So,' said Molly. 'They know something about green mice we don't.'

They wheeled the trolley to the kitchen, but paused outside, hearing voices.

'You have not taken sufficiently of it!' Imelda's voice was angry. 'Now is not the time to be jealous. Now is the time to take your medicine.'

They didn't hear Bryan's reply.

'Ah, now, Bryan darlink,' Imelda's voice was softer. 'Good. Drink it all, darlink.'

'Imelda!' It was Bryan. 'It makes me sick. Are you sure you know about this stuff?'

'Of course. Professor Leef said to …'

There was a splurting sound as Bryan spat out the medicine.

'*Him!* That old duffer!'

Joe was leaning harder and harder on the trolley as he strained to hear, and suddenly his weight sent it catapulting into the kitchen with a thunderous rattle.

'Isn't anywhere safe from you?' cried Bryan. 'What d'you mean by barging in here?'

'Sorry. Sorry,' Joe mumbled.

'It is nothink,' said Imelda. 'Carry on. I am outgoink.'

Bryan sank down into a chair like a deflated balloon as she went out. 'Oh, don't rattle those plates, kids. God, I'm sick.'

'You look a bit green,' Molly said.

'I feel green. I feel awful. She said it'd make me feel better. It doesn't. Now she says he told her to give it to me, that Professor Leef. They've tricked me.'

He lifted up his left hand and held it in front of his face. It was shaking. Slowly he hauled himself out of the chair and dragged himself upstairs, moaning as he went.

Chapter Seven

SAPP

On Thursday morning, before anyone else in the house was awake, and the garden was just coming to life with birdsong, Joe and Molly were back at the pool.

'It looks higher than it really is,' said Joe, who was sitting on the wall. 'About three metres. It'll be fine,' he said cheerily. It wasn't the distance so much as the atmosphere of the place that spooked him.

Molly jumped down first.

'Phew! It's OK,' she called up softly. 'Just a bit rough on the skin.' She beckoned him. 'Come on!'

Joe stared.

Molly was standing with her back to the water and the water was moving. The leaves and rubbish were shifting and swaying and suddenly, a green hump, like a tyre, broke the surface behind her – then disappeared.

Joe put his hands together in pretend prayer. Oh, help! he thought. It's there. A real monster.

'Coming!' he called.

He scrambled down the wall and, taking Molly's arm, casually pulled her towards the wall.

'Keep away from the edge of the pool, hey?'

'OK.' Molly shivered. 'It's gruesome in here. Feel it? Horrible.'

Joe nodded. It was like there was ice creeping up through the soles of his feet and inching around his heart. His face hurt from his brave, frozen grin.

'Large areas of deep water can be scary and of course it's walled in, too – that can be frightening, specially for agoraphobic people and maybe we're agoraphobic and never knew,' he gabbled. 'And we're all alone ... and there's that peculiar whine the breeze makes in the trees, and the lapping of the water.' He shivered and dug his hands deep into the pockets of his fleece.

'No,' said Molly, staring at the swimming pool. 'There's more.'

There was something in the air, trapped there by the four walls. It was something Molly had never come across before; something Joe had briefly glimpsed in his mother.

It was despair.

There was a sudden movement in the pool and instantly they both shrank back against the wall as if dragged by a strong magnet.

'Look. *Look!*'

The leaves shuffled and slithered. There was the dull *plop* as bubbles burst; underwater paddling sounds like a fish; soft splashing, and then suddenly, something shot out of the water like a cork popping to the surface.

They couldn't move, they could only stare.

Its body was about the size of a walrus with a long neck supporting a small lizard-like head. But unlike a lizard, this creature had large intelligent brown eyes which were staring straight into theirs.

Below the water Joe caught sight of flippers and a long tail. Its shiny skin was the lush polished green of rhododendron leaves.

Molly and Joe hugged the wall.

'It *is* a dinosaur,' Molly managed to whisper. 'D'you think it can get out? Has it got legs?'

'Don't know. But it doesn't look dangerous.'

'Doesn't it?'

'No. It looks nice … You can tell … like Bingo,' said Joe, breathing out heavily. 'And it's looking at us.'

Still the monster went on staring at them.

'What shall we do?'

Joe shrugged, then impulsively took a step towards the creature. It jerked backwards, splashing.

'It's OK,' Joe told it, gently. 'I'm not going to hurt you. Molly, did you see? It's scared.'

'The *students*!' said Molly, grimly.

'Yes. It looks sick.'

Finally, the animal blinked its watery eyes, gave a small whimper, and slowly slipped back beneath the leaves and disappeared.

'We've got to tell someone,' said Molly, 'before it's too late. It might die, Joe. Dad'll know what to do.'

'OK.' Joe shivered, wrapping his arms around himself. He scanned the high walls and the locked gates. 'Uh, oh! Mol, we're stuck!'

'What?' Molly spun round anxiously. 'We've *got* to get out. Of course we can get out.' She looked around. 'That changing hut might do. We'll come out right near the house but no one'll be up yet.'

'OK.'

They couldn't help glancing inside the hut. There were bottles of chemicals, jars and test tubes. Packets, creams and cotton wool. Even metal instruments that looked like hospital equipment.

Molly held her arm out in front of Joe. 'Don't touch anything!'

They stared at the stuff, feeling queasy. Joe picked up a sheet of paper.

'Experiments,' he said quietly, leafing through the papers. 'They're using the animal for tests. SAPP – What's that mean? *Tissue samples, blood tests, skin analysis* ... Ugh!' He clutched his stomach. 'How *could* they?'

'But they're *botanists*,' said Molly, shaking her head. 'Oh, I hate them for this!'

'Me, too. Come on, let's get out of here.'

Molly climbed quickly up on to the roof and, checking there was no one watching, pulled herself astride the wall.

'Hurry, Joe, please!'

Joe scrambled over the wall. He was in such a flap; his mind racing, full of vivid pictures and sounds, he didn't hear the faint rattle as something fell from his pocket, he didn't even hear the familiar *clunk* as the dice collided on the floor.

Not realising the evidence they were leaving behind them, Molly and Joe set off for home. Neither of them spoke for a while, then Molly let out a big sigh. 'In there is so ...' She took a big breath. 'I mean I'm glad we're out. That thing, the creature, it's ...'

'I know. Totally sad.'

'Yes, just awful. Joe – I've got an idea,' said Molly as they neared the house. 'While they're asleep, we could get in the lab. I know where the spare key is.'

'What for?'

'I need to ... ' She looked away. 'I want to see if Dad knows anything. I'm sure he doesn't, but ... I know his computer password. It wouldn't take a minute to check it.'

Joe nodded. He was reluctant in case they were caught, but he knew Molly needed to. They unlocked the door and crept in.

'What a place!' said Joe, gazing round the lab. 'It's really great.'

'Money from Professor Leef,' said Molly grimly.

There were microscopes and peculiar machines with numbers flashing and blinking as well as the computers. Rows of test tubes glinted in racks, glass bottles containing weird plant specimens lined the walls along with shelves of books.

Molly turned on her father's personal computer.

'What's his password?' asked Joe.

'Chlorophyll.'

'Chloro – who?'

'*Chlorophyll*, the pigment that makes plants green. It traps the light and turns water and minerals into energy.'

'Oh, *that* chlorophyll.'

Molly tried to open a file. 'It won't let me in!

It's asking for another password.'

'He must have changed it.'

Suddenly the computer chimed: *bing-bong-bing.*

'We have mail!' she cried in a loud whisper. 'Let's see if we can read it ... Yeah! It's from Professor Leef.'

She read it aloud.

```
Don't bother me here again. You will
lose every penny of your funding if I
hear one more word from you. It was a
mistake to let that boy come. If you
want to keep your funding and your good
reputation, you must let Imelda finish
her work. I'm warning you. If you
jeopardise this project I will tell the
Research Foundation everything.
```

'What does it mean?' whispered Molly. 'Tell the Foundation what?'

'Don't know.'

'And Dad'll see it's been read now. What shall we do?'

'Delete it,' said Joe. 'He won't miss *that*.'

Molly did as he said and turned off the computer.

'Blackmail,' she said quietly. 'But what could Dad have done wrong? Why would the Foundation stop his funding?'

'Perhaps we should ask him,' said Joe. 'I mean, you know your dad, Molly, he's a *good* man.'

'OK,' agreed Molly. 'We'll do it first thing.'

Chapter Eight
Bingo the Psychic

Joe went back to bed and slept until ten-thirty. He hurried downstairs when he saw the time, anxious to tell Dr Martin everything – but Mrs McBride was busy at the sink. Joe ate breakfast quickly and then he and Molly went out to the little summerhouse to talk.

'Where's your dad? Have you told him yet?'

'He's gone to see Professor Leef,' said Molly bleakly. 'I'm worried, Joe.'

'Shh! Someone's coming!'

They peeped out of the window. It was Bryan: strolling by, casually tossing … Joe's dice.

Joe smacked his empty pockets. 'My dice! Damn. Sorry, Mol. Now they *must* know we went in … What shall we do?'

They spent ten minutes trying to decide a course of action. Then Mrs McBride walked by.

Molly glanced at her watch. 'Where's she going? She's only just come!' She flung open the summerhouse door.

'Oh, Molly!' Mrs McBride looked flustered. 'That Imelda says I've to go home. I checked with your dad on the phone, so I'm off early.'

'*Dad* said you had to go?'

'Yes. I don't like leaving you with them, I must say, but I expect the doctor will be home soon.'

Mrs McBride patted Molly's arm, then marched out of the gate. Bingo trotted down the path after Mrs McBride then galloped back to the summerhouse, wagging his tail.

Joe shut the door firmly. 'I wish your dad would hurry back.'

'Me too. Why did he tell Mrs McB to go?' Molly mused. 'We must tell him about the animal – and what if Professor Leef asked Dad about that e-mail and Dad said, "What e-mail?" Then we're finished, Joe.'

Joe shrugged. 'Maybe. I don't think so. We'll act as if nothing's wrong. You ring Professor Leef and ask to speak to your dad.'

'But I'm scared. We *know* they know we were in the pool.'

'But *they* don't know *we* know they know,'

said Joe, grinning. 'And that is where our power lies, just like with magic, see. Keep the audience looking at the wrong thing, divert their attention, just until Uncle Rob comes home.'

Bryan was sitting at the table in the backyard, having a coffee.

'Hi! Do you want to see my new trick?' Joe said, brightly.

Bryan swatted a greenfly on the back of his hand. 'Go on then, squirt, a trick can't hurt, can it?'

'This is a really good one,' said Joe, placing three large, flowered eggcups upside down on the table. He put a coin under one then swirled them across the table.

'Find the coin!'

Bryan pointed. 'There.'

'Afraid not!' said Joe, lifting the eggcup. 'Try again.'

Bryan tried again and again.

'It's too quick!' He yelled at Imelda as she came out of the lab. 'It was there! It's gone!'

'What is happenink?' said Imelda, coldly.

'It's just a bit of fun, Imelda,' said Bryan. 'Look. See if you can find the coin. I can't.'

Joe swirled the cups around. 'Pick one.'

'There is no mices?' said Imelda, furtively touching a cup.

'No.'

Imelda put out her hand towards the end cup,

then paused. 'Does your psychic know the answer?'

'Of course.'

'Let him do it.'

Bingo jumped up and pushed his nose against the middle cup.

'That one,' said Joe.

Imelda lifted the cup and screamed: underneath was a white mouse.

'What?' Joe leapt up.

The mouse scampered off into the shrubbery with Bingo racing after it, barking wildly.

'You tricked me, you nasty boy!' snapped Imelda, breathing hard. 'I am tellink you I am not likink these creatures and you are trickink me!'

'I didn't mean to,' said Joe.

Imelda glared fiercely at him. 'I will pay you front for this.'

'Pay you *back*,' corrected Bryan automatically.

Imelda stalked over to the laboratory. 'Come, Bryan. Now. There is many thinks we must do.'

The door slammed behind them, just as Molly appeared.

'Phew! Say, where did that mouse come from?' said Joe. 'I've lost lots but never *found* them. It's crazy. I wish I *had* done it on purpose, though,' he added, smiling. 'Did you see Imelda's face ... Oh, Molly, what is it?'

Molly sank down beside him.

'When I rang Professor Leef, it was …' She rubbed her eyes and blinked hard. 'It was bad,' she sniffed. 'He was so cold. Said Dad wouldn't be coming home for a while. They're looking into his records and his books or something. Like Dad was a criminal. *Not coming home for a while*. What's *a while*, Joe?'

A chill rippled up Joe's spine. He shook his head.

They stared at each other.

'They sent Mrs McBride away and they've got Dad. They know we know about the animal. Joe, I think we should ring the police, I really do.'

Joe went from cold all over, to hot.

'The police? I suppose you're right. But don't mention the green thing – no one will believe that.'

'OK,' said Molly. 'Dad being Dad, we've no mobile. The safest would be the phone in the music room.'

Feeling like criminals, they crept into the house. Molly sat down on the window seat, wrapping the curtain round her, picked up the receiver and dialled nine-nine-nine. Joe watched anxiously. Molly's eyes widened in panic. She hit the phone against the seat.

'It's not working!' she whispered. 'Dead.'

'What? It was working a minute ago.'

Joe grabbed the phone from her and listened too. The silence was huge.

'They've cut us off. I was wrong: they do know we know they know.'

'We've got to get out of here. Now,' said Molly, jumping up, 'the nearest house is on the corner. You know, where Mrs Brigden lives with that little Jack Russell? She's the sort to believe us.'

'OK. The front door? Then they won't see us from the lab.'

They got to the door, were standing on the tiled floor, Molly's hand on the brass handle, when Joe turned to her, slapped his forehead and said, '*Bingo!* Molly, we can't go without Bingo!'

Chapter Nine
Trapped

'Where is he?'

'The mouse, remember? He was chasing it.'

'He's in the garden, then,' Molly said.

Joe knew she wanted to run. 'Molly, we *can't* leave him.'

Molly took a big breath. 'OK, look, we've got to pretend nothing's the matter so they don't suspect. We'll call for him, just as if we're going for a walk or something, grab him and then go. All right?'

'Yeah,' mumbled Joe, 'only … I have this really, really, bad feeling …' He gritted his teeth, tried to swallow the lump in his throat. 'He's *always* with me.'

They went back, tiptoed across the yard, past

the silent lab. 'He's never done this before. He never leaves me,' Joe muttered. The pain in his chest was so terrible he thought he would burst.

Whistling softly for Bingo, they crept to the greenhouses and checked inside: nothing.

Joe stared at Molly without really seeing her.

'*They've* got him,' he said. 'I know it. I can't leave … But *you* could go Molly …'

Molly shook her head.

'No, listen, it makes sense,' Joe insisted. 'Run to …' He stopped, head cocked on one side, like a bird. 'Did you hear? *Barking!*'

'Phew!' Molly grinned. 'Yes! He's OK, Joe.'

They ran towards the sound.

'The pool door's open!' Joe called as he ran in, then screeched to a halt.

Imelda.

Imelda stood there like a statue, cold, immobile, her cut-glass eyes glittering maliciously.

'*Molly!* Stop!' Joe yelled. But it was too late.

As Molly followed him in, Bryan stepped from behind the door and closed and locked it.

'We've been waiting,' he said. 'Nice of you kids to join us.'

They were trapped.

Imelda was staring at Joe like a cat might stare at a cornered rat.

'Walked straight into it,' smirked Bryan, cuffing Joe around the head. 'That was dumb, wasn't it?'

Joe and Molly stood side by side; they didn't speak.

Joe stared past Imelda to where Bingo scratched and whined from within a metal cage.

I mustn't let on I'm scared, Joe told himself. A good magician never panics, even when the tricks go wrong, even when the mice disappear, and the dove flies off. Keep calm.

'We knew you'd come,' said Bryan, folding his arms. 'When they realise they've lost that damn dog, I said to Imelda, then they'll come.'

'What do you want?' Joe said in a small voice.

'No questions. Come here!' snapped Imelda.

Neither Joe nor Molly moved.

'Come here now or watch me throwink that dog into that water!' Imelda screamed.

They scuttled over to her and let Imelda tie their hands and push them to the floor beside Bingo.

I bet Mol blames me for this, Joe thought, pushing his fingers through the cage bars. And it *is* all my fault, but I could never leave you, Bingo.

'Not scared, are you, kids?' Bryan's voice cracked and he coughed. He stumbled on the uneven paving stones. 'Stupid kids.'

'Listen,' said Imelda. 'I am only once sayink this to you. You interfered with our important experiment, now you must pay.'

'That's right,' Bryan agreed.

'Since you are messink this experiment all to pieces, we must move quickly,' said Imelda. 'We are needink a human guinea pink to test it out.'

'Human guinea *pig*,' amended Bryan, wearily.

'Guinea pig?' Molly whispered, colour draining from her cheeks as if someone had pulled a plug out.

'Yes. I must know it works.'

'What works? What do you want us to do?' asked Molly.

'Just take somethink. A chemical ... nothink dangerous.'

'And if we don't?'

Imelda looked pointedly at Bingo and shrugged.

'Then Bingo is going swimmink,' she said slowly. 'In his cage.'

'No!' Joe shook his head furiously. 'Tell me. I'll do it.'

'Take the SAPP.'

'SAPP?'

'It is from that thing.' She nodded towards the swimming pool. 'The final distillation. Too late for more samples because, anyways, the Planimal is dyink,' said Imelda. 'No more time.'

'Planimal?'

Bryan interrupted. 'Yes, "planimal". Half-plant, half-animal, you see? SAPP is the stuff we get out of it: Scientifically Animal and Plant Product. The thing's green. Makes its own food from the sun like a plant, but looks like an animal! A swimming cabbage! An aquatic aubergine!' and he laughed, but that brought on a fit of coughing and he had to sit down. 'Imelda doesn't understand,' he added in a tired voice. 'That SAPP, it's worth millions. I wanted to ...'

'Shut up!' said Imelda. 'I am knowink so much more than you. Be quiet!'

'OK, OK,' said Bryan.

'Isn't it a dinosaur?' asked Joe.

'*Planimal!*' snapped Imelda.

'But you're missing the point, Imelda,' said Bryan in a flat voice. 'See, Joe, we could put SAPP into ordinary people and turn them into *human plants*! A green person would have no need to eat. Imagine! There wouldn't be any need for food production, so no farms! All that land free for housing! No supermarkets. It means people could go and live in the desert or the deepest jungle and never worry about needing to eat. They'd just make their own food, for free! It could make us rich!'

'But it sounds horrid,' said Molly. 'There wouldn't be any farmers. No cows and no milk. No fields with wheat in. No flour. No bread. No ice cream.'

'It's more important than *ice cream*!' cried Bryan. 'It's the greatest discovery since, since, photosynthesis itself.'

'Shut up!' said Imelda. 'You know nothink.'

'Right,' said Bryan. 'Yes.' He put his arm around Imelda but she shrugged him off.

'Enough of this talkink and this explainink, please,' Imelda said. 'Who cares about the farms and the food? I just want the SAPP for *me*. Now, Joe, take the SAPP or I will kill this dog. I don't care. You are knowink that I don't care,' she added, flatly. 'It means nothink to me.'

'OK! OK!' yelled Joe.

'You can't, Joe!' cried Molly. 'It could be poisonous!'

Joe shook his head. 'I have to. You heard.'

'What will the SAPP do to him?' asked Molly.

'Same as the mouse,' said Bryan. 'He'll go green.'

Joe met Molly's eyes. 'So that's where the green mouse came from,' he said.

'Then what?' asked Molly.

Bryan paused. 'We'll test him, examine him – you don't need to know.'

'I'll be fine,' said Joe. 'So I'll go a bit leafy.' His voice trembled. 'Well ... I like vegetables.'

'Stop trying to be brave, Joe!' shouted Molly. 'Bryan, you can't do this, you can't!'

Bryan shrugged. 'Imelda insists.'

Imelda laughed. 'Don't worry, he'll be doing magic again very soon – if he's lucky.'

'I *am* lucky,' said Joe, firmly. 'I'm a very lucky person, I've got a lucky dog, lucky dice ...'

'Come here.'

'Joe, don't!'

'I've got to.' Joe sat on the chair. He looked into Bingo's brown, trusting eyes. 'I must.'

Imelda came out of the shed with a cloth-covered tray.

'This is it,' said Imelda, picking up a small bottle from the tray. '*Green* SAPP! Yellow first and not workink so well.'

Joe and Molly exchanged a worried look. Bryan had taken the yellow stuff. Bryan wasn't working so well, either. Joe swallowed nervously.

Imelda unscrewed the bottle and squeezed the rubber bulb in the lid. 'Three drops only,' she told Joe.

Right, thought Joe. Three drops only. OK. Be brave. Be lucky.

Everything grew suddenly very quiet and still. The wind died down.

Bingo stopped whining.

Molly held her breath.

Bryan sniggered.

'Out stick your tongue,' said Imelda.

Joe started to giggle nervously. It sometimes happened when he was about to start a magic show: he'd start giggling and then the audience laughed too and it made the show go really well, but this wasn't a show and his audience wasn't laughing.

'I don't expect it will work,' said Joe, forcing a chuckle, forcing a smile. 'Me, go green? I don't even go brown in the summer.'

'The tongue!'

Joe did as she asked. Suddenly he got a whiff of a terrible smell. He coughed, was about to complain, when he felt a cold tasteless drop on his tongue, then it slithered down his throat.

'Ugh!'

'Shh. Again!'

The second drop slipped down. That one tasted green, he thought, it really did. Like freshly mown grass. Like trees.

'Will it make me feel any differ—?'

The third drip fell coldly on to his tongue.

Without warning, Joe found he was sliding through a great green jelly, cushioned by soft mossy greenness, surrounded by emerald light. His head was filled with green; there was green juice coursing through his veins, all around was the smell of crushed leaves and newly mown grass.

Chapter Ten
Green

Much later, Joe came slowly to his senses.

His first thought, just as on most mornings, was of his mother. Was she all right? Would she get up today? No, there was something more important now ... Bingo in a cage! The cold drops on his tongue ... the green smells. Then he remembered ...

He'd taken the SAPP.

He opened his eyes and blinked. He seemed to be looking through thick glasses which made everything blurred and patched with green.

He looked down at his hands to see if he could untie them. Whoops! They were green. He was as green as a grasshopper.

Agh! A wave of horror washed over him and

sent his heart hammering.

Steady on! Get a grip, he told himself. Of course I'm green. Of course, what did you think, you idiot? They *wanted* you to go green and you *have* gone green, like that mouse.

He dared himself a second look. His hand was like a horse-chestnut leaf fanned out before him, green with prominent pale green veins.

I'm a *planimal*! Scientifically Animal and Plant. That's me. *Green Fingers.* The new magician with branches for arms. Will you still love me, Mum, if you have to keep me in a tank of water like that creature? And what'll they say at school? I'll never make the football team …

A tear escaped from his eye and Joe licked it as it trickled beside his mouth. Was that green too? Tastes a bit like spinach.

'Help!' he yelled. 'Help!'

There was something very wrong there. That shout wasn't right at all. He tried again. 'Help!'

Nothing had come out. He had no voice.

Well, who's ever heard of a talking rose? A chatty iris? Oh, this is bad, very bad …

Suddenly he stopped. He'd heard something.

Cautiously, Joe opened his eyes again. He peered down the length of the greenhouse. No one. So *who* could he hear?

He lay very, very still.

It was minuscule whispering sounds that he

could hear, almost like leaves rustling. It was getting louder and stronger.

Who was it? Where were they?

As Joe concentrated on the sounds, they began to form pictures in his head.

'Sunshine, warm, yellow, gold.'

'Dry, crinkly, crunch. Snap, crisp, crack. Dry.'

'Plush, moist, squidge, plump.'

'Green. Green. Green.'

Joe felt it all: the dryness, crisp and crackling inside him, then the water as it seeped through him, plumping up his veins, racing around his body like sap. And he could feel *green*: the deepest green of dark pine forests, the soft yellow green of emerging baby leaves, shiny purple green of rubbery leaves, and bright emerald green of pond weed. Dazzling.

Slowly, it dawned on Joe that he was hearing the plants; the plants in the greenhouse were *talking* to each other.

If only Uncle Rob could hear this! thought Joe. It would be the best treat ever for a botanist to hear his plants! But I can't lie here listening to this for ever. I've got to get free.

Something tickled his cheek.

A green ribbon was dangling over his nose. No, not a ribbon, it was a tendril from a climbing plant.

They're growing over me, like ivy, he thought

miserably. I'll disappear beneath them, like a ruined house. Go away! Get off!

The tickling tendril stopped tickling.

Joe froze: had he actually talked to a plant?

He looked up at the pale green tendril, it was moving, slowly shaping itself into an elegant arrow: pointing at something …

A pair of secateurs!

Freedom! Oh, thank you! I'll never say a bad word about a plant ever again, Joe promised. I'll even say nice things to spinach. And swede.

As Joe's fingers closed around the sharp secateurs, a tremor passed through him and ricocheted through the plants, like a frightened breeze.

'Hew, hack, slash!'

'Chop, split, carve!'

I won't hurt you, Joe promised. I won't touch you.

Quickly, he cut through the string on his wrist. A few seconds later he had the strength to sit up and cut free his feet too. But he was weak.

I need a drink. I need the light. I need to get out of here.

He dragged himself out of the greenhouse, breathing in the fresh air gratefully, but his legs buckled under him like fragile stalks and he fell on to the grass. Weedy, he thought, I'm weedy. I suppose plants aren't designed to move.

He managed to reach the rain bucket beside the door and gulped water greedily, then sprawled on the earth like a shipwrecked sailor.

The sun warmed his skin and he smiled. It was good. The sun was so yellow, so hot and the light was penetrating his skin and into his blood, he could feel it, powering him up like a battery charger. Energy zapped through his body like electricity. He felt incredible!

Joe grinned. Was that me saying plants were boring? This is that thing: photosynthesis. I'm doing it. I'm making my own energy from the sunlight. It's great. It's weird.

Now I know what Grandma means – she says my visits cheer her, she calls me a *tonic*. This is a tonic. This feeling ... Hey! *Mum* needs a tonic and she loves flowers ... If I could get her this feeling, well, that might do it! That might get her out of bed!

His idea was exciting. He rolled over and over in the grass, chortling soundlessly.

Yes, yes! If I get out of this all right, with Molly and Bingo OK ... If I can just get some more SAPP, then Mum'll hear the flowers too, she'll make her own energy, and get out of bed. She will. I know she will.

Chapter Eleven
The Planimal

Joe staggered to the first tree, a giant cedar, and held it tightly. He loved that tree. He loved all trees. Then slowly he set off towards the pool, touching the leaves, nodding hello at the bushes, a big grin splitting his face.

The pool. All was silent as he crept through the door. Nobody. Yes! Bingo! Bingo scrabbling in his cage, his entire body wagging with glee at the sight of his master.

Oh, Bingo! Bingo! Quickly Joe set him free. He stroked his ears, rubbed his head and his tummy; they rolled on the floor in a silent frenzy of adoration, then suddenly Bingo stopped. Joe stopped. He spun round. Someone was there.

It was the Planimal.

It had risen silently right beside them, sad eyes staring straight into Joe's. Droplets of water dripped and rolled over its green dome-shaped back, glistening like jewels. It whimpered softly.

Joe felt like running, and he felt like throwing his arms round its green neck and kissing it. He swallowed against the lump which crammed his throat. The sadness. The despair.

What do you want? Joe asked, silently. *What? I know you're not dangerous,* Joe told the Planimal, edging forward. *I know you're just like me. Can you hear my plant voice? Can I help you?*

The creature was an arm's length from him. So near. Bingo inched forward bravely, sniffing this strange new smell.

Tentatively, Joe held out his hand, took one step closer. The Planimal glided towards him, hesitated, looking inquiringly into Joe's eyes, paddled forward again, closer, so close, then lay its head against Joe's open palm, softly, trustingly, the way Bingo might.

Joe trembled, awed at the creature's faith in him.

He felt the weight of its head, wondered briefly if it had sharp teeth, was aware of its warmth and its smooth skin like a frond of seaweed. Then the Planimal began to hum.

It was a soft noise, no louder than a bee, but not like a bee buzzing busily from flower to flower; this was the hum of a machine on the blink. How crazy, it reminded him of his mum; of those first days when she was ill and would stand on the back doorstep, gazing at nothing and humming, droning more like. Awful.

The Planimal's hum grew into a whine and a whimper and a sad, low, keening wail and Joe began to see things.

Later when Joe tried to tell Molly about it, he found it very hard to explain how the vivid pictures had filled his head. A long, narrow lake. A ruined castle built of honey-coloured stone. Fields behind it. Low trees reaching down to the shore. Was it home?

Then pain. Suffering. Hurt. *They'd* hurt it and it was very sick.

I'll get you out of here, somehow, Joe promised. He stroked the animal's head encouragingly until the Planimal slowly dipped under the leaves and disappeared.

Joe was about to go, when some tiny movement in the shed, caught his eye. He turned sharply, fearing Imelda, but it was a small cage full of mice. Joe guessed the students must have been using them, and swiftly picked them up.

You'd better come with me. Don't want you turned green or used up in some other hideous experiment!

Chapter Twelve
Yellow SAPP

'You!' Joe almost leapt on Bryan and throttled him with his bare hands. Then he paused: Bryan was sick.

He was draped loosely over a garden bench, like a wet sock, his eyes were closed and he was hardly breathing.

Bryan lifted his head slightly, squinting up at Joe as if the sun hurt his eyes. He grinned feebly.

'Joe. Joe, good to see you, kid.'

Bryan looked like he was decaying: skin mottled green and yellow; hair lank and lifeless. His body seemed boneless, giving no substance to his clothes, he was as flat as as a piece of folded paper, his dangling hands trembled like leaves teased by the breeze.

'Well, just look at you!' Bryan croaked. 'Spinach-face! Hah!'

Joe bit his lip.

'Imelda did it.' Bryan closed his eyes again. 'She *used* me. It was never vitamin tonic, that foul yellow stuff in the bottle, remember? It was SAPP.'

Joe gulped. If the yellow SAPP did *that* to Bryan, what would the green SAPP do to him?

'Don't worry,' said Bryan, reading his thoughts. 'You got the green SAPP. It's better. They double-crossed me, but they'll be the losers. Joe, use the SAPP and get rich!'

Joe shook his head.

'Nah? Ah, well, show us a trick, Joe … Here's your dice.' He held them out on his palm and Joe took them quickly.

Bryan slipped further down the bench and his foot tipped out of his shoe.

'Something in my sock,' he muttered, struggling to peel down his sock with his other foot. 'Must be a stone, in my sock, something …'

Joe was glad that Bryan couldn't see what was in his sock.

It wasn't stones at all. From all over Bryan's pale feet, long grey, worm-like protrusions were growing: roots, burrowing into the earth.

'Shan't be going far now,' murmured Bryan.

Something dreadful was happening to his

face, too: it was getting flatter and flatter, like a giant mottled leaf.

'Rooted to the spot, am I? Ah, water. Sunshine. Warmth ...'

Joe ran, gripping the cage of mice against his chest.

'It won't happen to me. It won't happen to me!' he chanted. 'My SAPP was green. I'll be OK. Cool. I can't go like Bryan, I can't!'

* * *

As Joe neared the house, he heard screams and the noise of splintering glass. Spilled powders and liquids, papers and test tubes were strewn across the yard.

The students' car was beside the lab door, packed, ready to go. Imelda. Escaping with the SAPP.

How can I stop her? Joe thought desperately. Why can't I *really* do magic? If only I'd finished book three with that trick to make mice appear, she hates mice ... Hang on ... I've *got* mice ...

Quickly, he undid the cage and tipped the mice into the car.

'And now, ladies and gentlemen, for my final performance tonight, we have the multiplying mice trick. With one flick of my magic wand and one flutter of my magic hanky ...'

Bingo barked a warning, but too late.

Joe jumped and spun round.

'Get away from my car!' screamed Imelda.

Uh oh! Go, Bingo! Joe willed the dog to leave. *Quickly, get out of here!*

Psychic, for once, Bingo scampered inside the house, barking furiously.

Imelda marched towards him carrying bundles of papers and boxes. And the bottle of SAPP.

'Move away, guinea pink. What? Can't speak? Shame.' She waved the small green bottle. 'SAPP. Thank you so much for tryink it. It will be savink my life.'

Joe looked puzzled.

'How, eh? The Professor and I, we had experiment. First we try on Bryan. Didn't work. But now I know this SAPP will keep me so young and so lovely. Yes, is clever man, my professor. You are not believink me?' she said, seeing Joe's puzzled expression. 'But you are the one looking so closely all the time. You see the lines and stitches. Look!'

Smiling like a crocodile, she slowly took hold of her hair and pulled.

Joe closed his eyes.

'Look! Look,' she insisted and Joe looked.

Imelda's lovely long, blonde hair hung lifelessly in her hand. Imelda laughed, stroking her shiny smooth white scalp.

'Some steel, some titanium.' She fingered the tiny bolts and metal plates on her head. 'After accident I am a bit of a mess. Professor puts me back like this. Still parts of me organic and they need SAPP. Now I live for ever! More beautiful every day!'

She stuck her hair back on and stepped towards the car.

'Goodbye,' she said, opening the car door, 'it was ... Aaaaargh!'

She screamed as a great tidal wave of mice tumbled out over her, squirming and squeaking, running in every direction. They covered her entire body, like a living fur coat.

Joe shook his head in astonishment.

Maybe it's all those hundreds of mice lost by all the hundreds of magicians suddenly coming to help? Or maybe it's the magic of being green.

Imelda staggered backwards, swiping wildly at the mice and suddenly the bottle of SAPP flew from her hand.

Yeah! Joe rushed for it.

Imelda saw him coming and stuck out her arms to grab him, but just at the last moment, Joe ducked and dived between her legs, and she grabbed thin air. He swooped on the bottle of SAPP and picked it up as if he were scooping up a rugby ball, and ran.

Where?

The car door was hanging invitingly open and he dived inside. Phew, safe.

Chapter Thirteen
Imelda

Joe quickly pressed down the door-lock and slipped the bottle of SAPP into his pocket. Putting his hands on the steering wheel, he fantasised for a second about driving off and then noticed his hands were less green. The SAPP was wearing off. No more magic, then.

Imelda was peeling mice from her clothes and flinging them off. She banged on the window, bringing him to his senses.

'It is *my* SAPP!' she yelled. 'Give it to me. I'm not askink Joe, I am *tellink* you!'

When Joe shook his head, Imelda glared at him fiercely, then marched across to the hose pipe and turned it on.

'I am needink that stuff. For my beauty. Be

out of that car now or I will drown you dead!'

Joe shook his head.

'Foolish boy!'

Imelda opened the bonnet of the car and vanished momentarily from sight. Nervously, Joe sat listening to the clunking and banging sounds from the front of the car. Seconds later, water began to flood around his feet. She really was planning to drown him dead! What use was his mystery and illusion now? Magic wasn't going to help him out of this.

The water rose fast.

Joe scooped up a brown mouse which was swimming furiously around the brake pedal and placed it safely on the seat. The water crept quickly up his legs and over the seat.

'Somebody *do* something!' he begged. 'Help!' His voice had come back.

Imelda put her face up to the window and grinned in at him.

'Soon you will be drownink,' she said sweetly. 'The dear little furry mices will be floatink on their little furry backs with little pink paws in the air ... Drowned dead!'

The water was up to his neck. The mice were squeaking, the water was swirling and gurgling around him ...

'One! Two! Three!' he yelled, and dived for the door handle. The weight of the water swung the door open really fast and Joe, mice and papers tumbled out in a heap.

'Aha! Got you!' cried Imelda, grabbing and twisting his arm in a vice-like grip. 'The SAPP! Give it now!'

'OK. OK. Let me go. I can't reach it.'

'No tricks, Mr Magic,' she warned, relaxing her hold.

He felt in his pocket. 'It's gone.'

'Liar!' She threw him on to the ground.

They both saw the bottle at the same time. It had fallen out and been whisked away in the flood and now it was lying near the drain bobbing as water washed under it.

Imelda and Joe both lunged towards it. Imelda was the quickest, but her foot caught in the hose pipe – she tripped, knocking Joe to the ground and sending the hose swinging round, jetting water straight at the bottle.

Helplessly they watched as the tiny bottle was flung up and over and disappeared down the drain.

'No! No,' whispered Joe. 'Now Mum'll never get better. Never feel that plant energy. Oh, Mum, I'm sorry!' He wiped his eyes fiercely.

Imelda stood above him with her hands on her hips.

Her lips were curled back over her perfect teeth, her silky hair hung like molten metal over her shoulders. Her eyes, icy as cut diamonds, sparkled viciously.

'You have ruinated everythink,' she hissed. She placed her foot on to Joe's ankle and leaned until the sharp gravel cut into him. 'You wasted my time. You lost the SAPP.' With each word she ground his ankle harder into the gravel. 'You have ruinated my life! Now I will ruinate yours!'

She reached into her pocket and took out a small black bottle. On the label was a skull and crossbones.

She's going to kill me, Joe thought. I'm dead. I'm truly dead.

'Stop! Stop!'

It was Molly. She and Bingo rushed out together and flung themselves at Imelda, knocking her off balance, sending her crashing against the wall. The bottle dropped from her hand and smashed, spraying liquid over a dandelion. Within seconds the flower shrivelled and died.

'Phew,' gasped Joe.

Suddenly, the sound of an engine surprised them all and Professor Leef's car sped into the yard with a screech of brakes and spray of pebbles.

'Imelda!' Professor Leef roared, staggering over to her and wrapping his plump arms around her. 'What's the matter? My poor lovely, darling. What is it?'

'They've taken the SAPP!' Imelda snarled. 'Kill them!'

The Professor held her gently. 'Now, now,' he crooned.

'The SAPP's gone,' said Joe. 'Lost.'

'It's really gone, honestly,' Molly said. 'Take her away. Please.'

Professor Leef nodded. 'We'll start again, my darling,' he whispered to Imelda, straightening her wig. 'We'll find another way. Don't worry. You will be beautiful. You are always beautiful to me.'

He helped Imelda into his car and they drove away.

* * *

'I lost the SAPP,' said Joe.

'It doesn't matter,' said Molly.

Joe opened his mouth to tell her why he'd wanted it so badly, then changed his mind. It had been a mad idea. He couldn't really help his mother. He covered his eyes with his hands.

'What's the matter?'

'Just tired.'

'I bet. See, Joe, I always said she'd had a facelift.'

'Yeah,' Joe nodded wearily, 'and that's why our counting trick went wrong, remember? Bingo only counted *real* people so he didn't include her.'

'Clever Bingo!'

'Yeah. Where is that clever Bingo?'

They found him scratching at the locked cellar door and hidden in the cellar they found Uncle Rob, tied to a chair.

'Dad!'

'Thank goodness!' Dr Martin gasped. 'Quick! Untie me. Hurry ...'

'It's OK,' said Joe, working on the knots. 'They've gone. It's over.'

Dr Martin blinked. 'Thank God!' he breathed, relaxing. 'Come on, let's get out of this dismal hole and you can tell me what happened.'

Joe quickly went and changed into some dry clothes. Then they sat down at the kitchen table and told the doctor everything. He especially wanted to know how Joe had felt being green.

'I felt weak at the beginning, but the sun gave me energy and the water sort of pumped out my legs! And I could hear the plants talking. I could hear the flowers and the grass ... I talked to the Planimal – oh, I'd forgotten about the Planimal. It's despairing. It'll die if we don't get it out.'

Uncle Rob sighed.

'Tell,' urged Molly. 'I want to know you had nothing to do with any of this.'

'Herrum, well,' her father began, 'I was examining water samples and one of them had this little animal in it ...'

'The Planimal?'

'Yes, it was about the size of a frog. I knew it was special, but not that special. When I realised that it was as much a plant as it was an animal, I was flabbergasted – and this is what caused all the trouble. I kept it *secret*. You see, I saw possibilities. Why not have green humans too?'

'You wanted to *experiment* on it?' said Molly.

'I wanted to *study* it. Thousands could benefit from such a discovery. Think of all those poor countries where crops are hard to grow! Turn their people green and they could just sit in the sun, drink water, eat the odd mineral and be fit and healthy, all for free!'

'Bryan knew that,' said Joe. 'He reckoned he'd be rich.'

'Exactly. In the wrong hands it was dangerous. That's why I couldn't go on with it.'

'Then?'

'Herrum, Bryan told Professor Leef. Leef said I'd kept it secret to make myself rich. Who'd believe I hadn't? I'd lose my funding, maybe my home. Then Leef sent in Imelda.'

Molly interrupted. 'Professor Leef said the SAPP would keep Imelda beautiful, like an elixir or something.'

'Possibly … I was on the verge of telling the Foundation everything when Leef kidnapped me!' went on Dr Martin. 'Leef is sure to lose his job – if he ever comes back, which I doubt. Come on, let's go to the lab. There are things I need to see.'

* * *

Dr Martin flicked through his files quickly, then typed in some numbers. 'We'll find where that creature really belongs.'

Molly peered at the screen.

'Loch Greenburn!' she said. 'Scotland. Is that like Loch Ness, then?'

Her father grinned. 'Herrum, I think it must be, my dear. You see those lochs are fearfully cold and deep: ideal for hiding a big animal. And a planimal would survive very well, making its own food, probably from a very low light intensity. Exciting, eh?'

'Sort of,' said Molly. 'Now can we take it home?'

* * *

By ten o'clock that night, the Planimal lay in a water-filled dinghy in the back of a borrowed van, its long neck draped like a limp snake over the boat's edge.

Joe and Molly took turns stroking it, but the Planimal hardly responded. Its eyes were growing misty.

All night they drove north and it was mid-morning by the time they arrived at the isolated, lonely Loch Greenburn. They piled out of the van, yawning and stretching, and shivering in the cold air.

Joe looked around, then burst out: 'The castle and the lake!' He pointed at them. 'Exactly what it showed me!'

Dr Martin got out, dragging on a thick coat. 'Good. Loch Greenburn's deep, maybe seven or eight hundred feet, plenty of room here.'

They opened up the back of the van.

'It knows where it is,' cried Joe, as the Planimal lifted its head, turned its big, sad eyes towards the water, and let out a throaty, vibrant cry.

They pulled it out of the dinghy, on to the marshy ground at the water's edge. Joe stroked its head as it gulped tiredly for air.

'Go on. You can do it,' he urged it gently.

Don't give up, he told it silently. *You can make it, you can, you can! If you do it, Mum will too. Go on.*

'Go on!' he almost shouted, pushing against the Planimal's wet and rubbery flanks.

Molly and Joe cupped the icy loch water in their hands and threw it over the Planimal's flanks.

'Can you feel that?' Joe shouted. 'It's your water! Go on!'

All at once, the Planimal lurched into the loch, ducked its head under the water and sort of tumbled under the surface, a flurry of flippers and bendy body, splashing and rolling.

Bingo burst into a volley of barks.

'Yes!' cried Joe, punching the air. 'Yes!'

Slowly, the Planimal swam out. When it was about fifty metres from shore it turned, looked long at them, as if committing their faces to memory, then sank beneath the water.

Joe couldn't speak. He found he'd been holding his breath for so long he felt quite faint. He sat down heavily and let Bingo snuggle into his arms.

Chapter Fourteen
Greening Mum

Three days later, Joe was back home. He followed his father up the path.

The garden looks so small, Joe thought. Just two little brown patches of soil on either side. No flowers. Even the hedge was leafless.

Uncle Rob had let Joe pick as many flowers as he'd wanted from the garden: a great bunch of daffodils and another of narcissi. At first Joe was anxious – surely it was bad to cut plants? But Uncle Rob assured him it was OK when the plants were appreciated.

'Hello, Mum,' he whispered.

She was sleeping. Her arms lay on top of the covers: very still, white and thin, like leafless winter branches, Joe thought.

Quietly, Joe placed the flowers around the room.

It looked wonderful. It looked really fine … But not green enough.

He called to Bingo and they went out into the back lane and cut long swathes of fresh greenery.

'What *are* you doing?' asked his dad.

'Greening Mum,' grinned Joe.

His dad grinned back. 'Never heard of it.'

Joe put the leafy branches on the bed cover. It would have been better if he had the SAPP, but still, the bedroom looked splendid now.

His mum was still asleep; didn't even know he'd come back.

Bingo jumped up and settled down at the foot of his mum's bed. The movement woke her and she opened her eyes and looked straight at a vase of daffodils.

'Oh,' she breathed.

'Hello, Mum. D'you like the flowers? I wanted to bring you this really special green medicine, but …' He placed her hand on a branch of Wych Elm, new leaves unfolding. 'I wish I could bring a whole tree in. Can you feel it, Mum, can you feel that energy? It wants to pull you out of bed. Wants to get you back the way you were.'

'Joe, dear Joe,' his mother murmured. She

put her other hand out and held his. 'It's so good to have you back.'

This was the most positive, the most *alive* she'd been for ages.

As Joe tiptoed out she started to hum: a rich, happy noise and she was smiling. Smiling.

Joe raced downstairs and out into the back garden.

'You OK?' his dad called through the kitchen window.

'I am,' said Joe. 'And so's Mum. Dad?'

'Yes?'

'We need to do something with this garden.'

'Do we?'

'Yes, we need to plant things in it. Make a really beautiful green place for Mum to sit in when she gets up. Hey, Dad we could have a little sun place here with one of those wooden decks and a trellis for climbing plants. We need to have everything green!'

'Do we, Joe?' laughed his father.

'Yes, we do,' said Joe.

About the Author

I am proud to say that I was born in Yorkshire, as were my parents and grandparents before me. I now live in Bristol, which is much warmer, with my husband, three boys and a dog and a cat. As a child growing up in a house with stone floors and no central heating, I was cold most of the time. I spent hours in bed with a hot water bottle, reading. I loved Enid Blyton and anthologies of fairy tales with pictures. When I ran out of books, or grew tired of what I had, I wrote and illustrated my own.

About Planimal Magic …

The rest of my family were artists. Just to be different, I chose biology. But when I got to university, biology involved cutting up and examining rather a lot of dead animals. Oh, those sad, glassy, reproachful eyes! Plants might mind just as much about being cut up, but at least they don't fix you with those eyes, so I switched to study botany. It was wonderful. Plants, I discovered, lead a secret beautiful life, on which all animal life depends. I was changed for ever. One day, mashing up some leaves into a green sludge in the lab, my chum dared me to drink the potion. Would I sprout leaves and start photosynthesising? The idea for *Planimal Magic* was born.

Black Cats – collect them all!

The Gold-spectre • Elizabeth Arnold
The Ramsbottom Rumble • Georgia Byng
Calamity Kate • Terry Deary
The Custard Kid • Terry Deary
Footsteps in the Fog • Terry Deary
The Ghosts of Batwing Castle • Terry Deary
Ghost Town • Terry Deary
Into the Lion's Den • Terry Deary
The Joke Factory • Terry Deary
The Treasure of Crazy Horse • Terry Deary
The Wishing Well Ghost • Terry Deary
A Witch in Time • Terry Deary
Planimal Magic • Rebecca Lisle
Eyes Wide Open • Jan Mark
Dear Ms • Joan Poulson
Spook School • Sue Purkiss
It's a Tough Life • Jeremy Strong
Big Iggy • Kaye Umansky
Quirky Times at Quagmire Castle • Karen Wallace
Something Slimy on Primrose Drive • Karen Wallace
Drucilla and the Cracked Pot • Lynda Waterhouse
Moonmallow Smoothie • Philip Wooderson